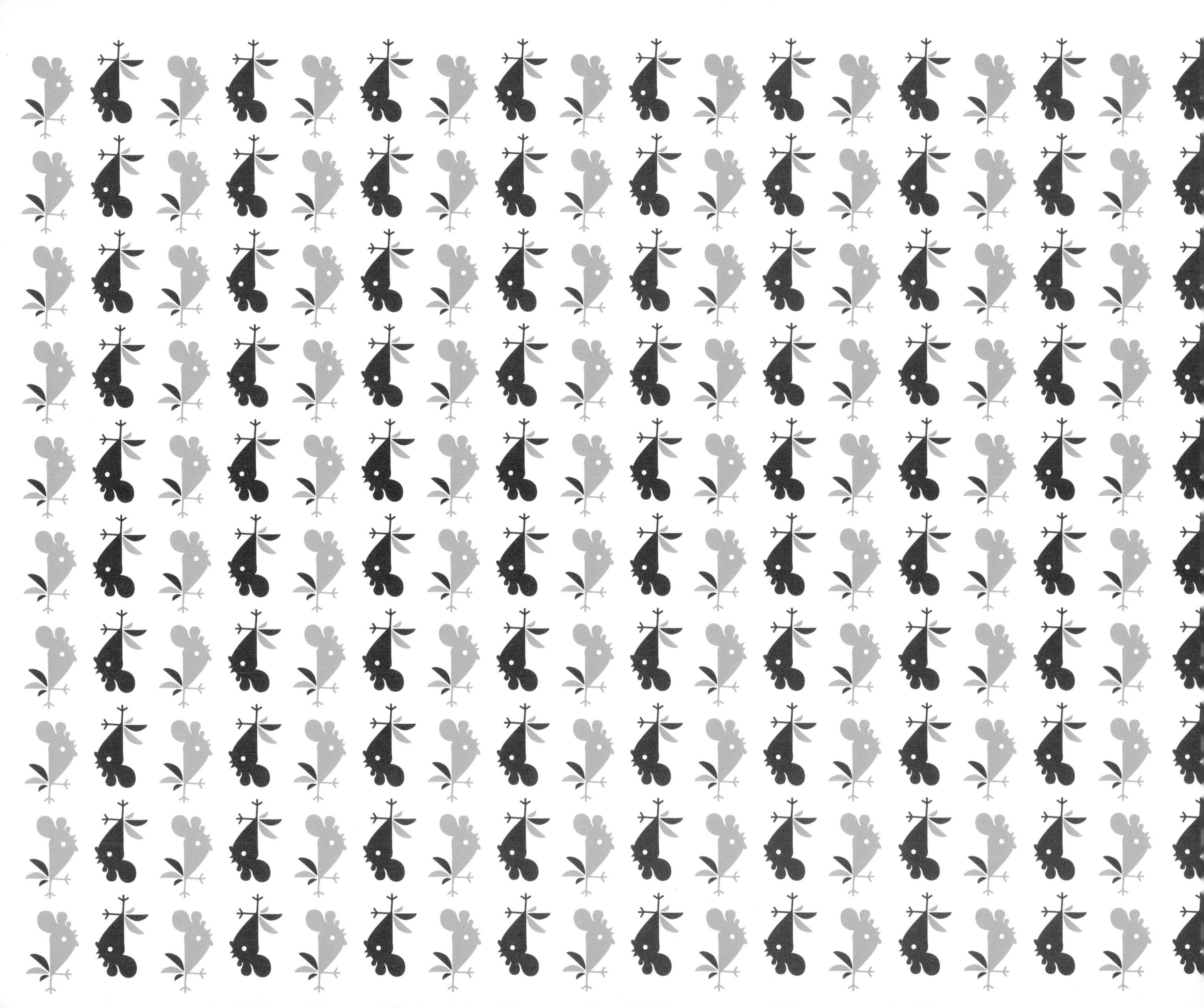

ISBN 978-1-338-24588-2

10 9 8 7 6 5 4 3 2 18 19 20 21 22

Printed in the U.S.A. 40

First printing 2018

CARLOS ZAMORA

Scholastic Inc.

Two little roosters
met at the park.

Tony said
¡Hola!

Charlie answered
What?!
32

I was just trying
to say hello.
Let's play some fútbol!
Uno, dos, tres ...
Go!

Do you mean
soccer?
Get it right, bro!

That's how I say it.
Hurry up, come on,
I'll teach you Spanish.
It will be fun!

They kept on talking, running around ...

and kicking the ball all over town.

Your Spanish is great,
I mean it – really –
but when I try to speak
I feel quite silly.

Languages are
like ice-cream scoops:
one is all right, but
two are awesome-good!

Think of new flavors,
music, and words ...

A whole new world
en español!

Playing in the alley,
Charlie kicked the ball.

To his surprise . . .

he scored a ...

COCKA

OODLEDOO

KiKiR

What was **that**, Tony?

Charlie, that's **me.**

Wow! What a crow! You're the coolest bird I know!

Here is the first word you need to learn:

Amigo ...

my friend!

This book is a celebration of friendship and identity,
a playful story about the value of bilingualism
and a reflection on the differences that bring us together.

CARLOS ZAMORA

is a Cuban American graphic designer and illustrator.
He lives between Saint Louis and La Habana with his wife Juliana,
daughters Aitana and Lucía, and a dog named Luna.
He used to take long walks with his *abuelo* Francisco on his way to school,
playing a game of counting imaginary banty roosters
out and about in the city.
This is his first picture book.

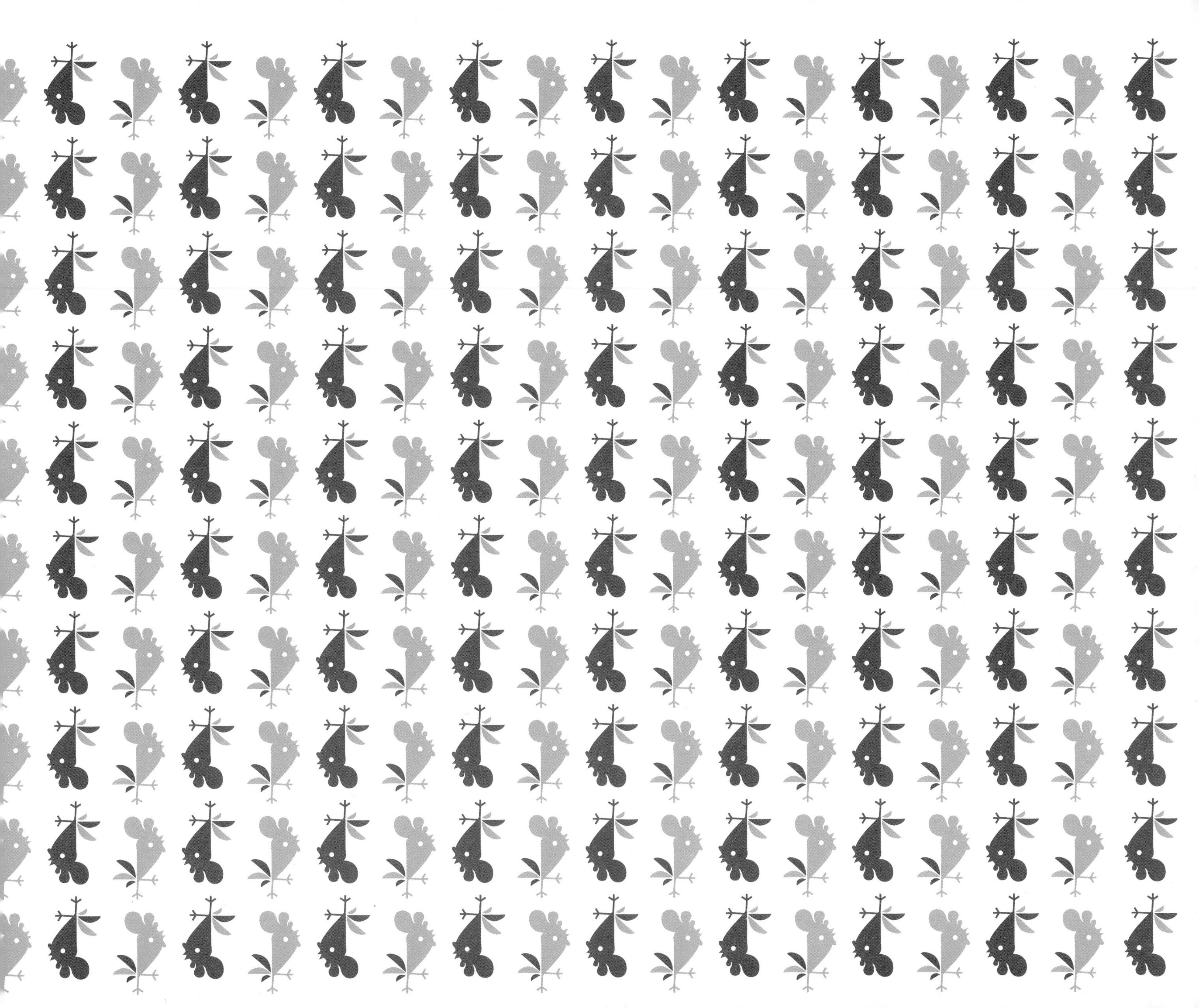

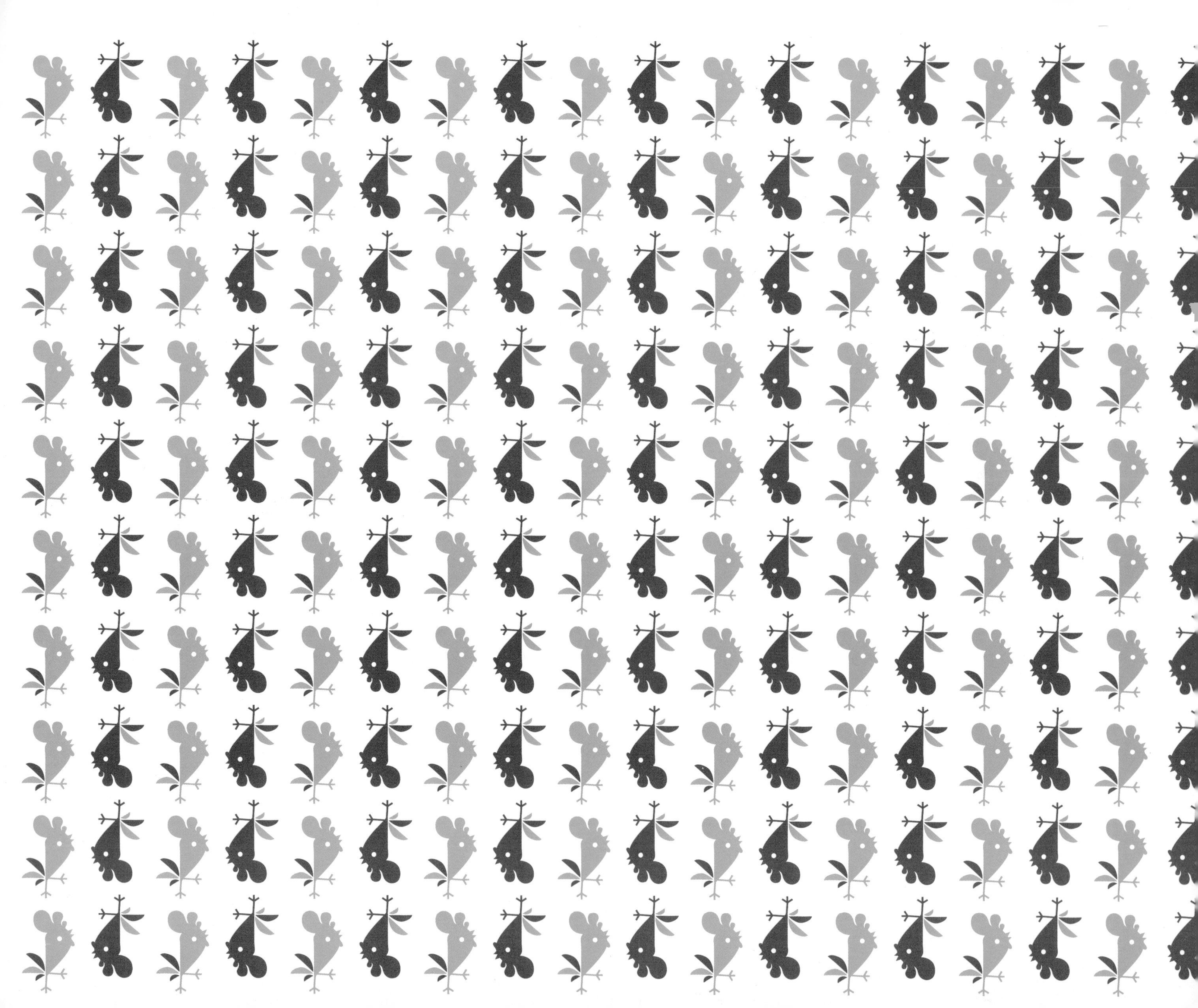